Anonymous

Jim and Nell: a dramatic poem in the dialect of North Devon

Anonymous

Jim and Nell: a dramatic poem in the dialect of North Devon

ISBN/EAN: 9783337304607

Printed in Europe, USA, Canada, Australia, Japan

Cover: Foto ©Andreas Hilbeck / pixelio.de

More available books at **www.hansebooks.com**

JIM AND NELL:

A Dramatic Poem

IN THE

DIALECT OF NORTH DEVON.

BY

A DEVONSHIRE MAN.

London:

PRINTED FOR PRIVATE CIRCULATION.

MDCCCLXVII.

JIM AN' NELL.

PEART I.

Scene, Guenerer Varm.

"CUM! daug et Will—Ott ar't about?
 An' dithn't muve, I'll gie th' a clout—
  Yen ma thick Cris'mus brawn:
An' dra' thick settle nigh tha clock,
An' auff tha brandis tak' tha crock,
  Yer's Maister a-cum haum.   ‑

"Doant strake about tha house, bit muve,
Tha stinpole lout!—'Od rat it you've
  Smál time to git things vitty:
Cum, doo be peart a-bit—tha mux
A-tap tha draxel's up ta hux,
  I'm vexed tha keaks be clitty.

"We've hailed tha neck, torned pegs ta arish,
We'm gwain ta zee up haff tha parish,
  Fegs, they'll be yer azoon;
Ott a gurt busker toad thee art!
I thort thee'st got et all by heart,
  Where have 'e clapped tha spūne?

" Jan, clare tha 'cess in t'other houze,
Vrom they old kex, an' bring tha browze,
   And cricks vrom Cockhedge plat ;
Muve, bloggy, clopping blindego !
Whare is voaks docity a-go ?
   They doant know ot be at.

" Giles, git zum stroyl out o' tha shippen,
And carr et down to tha bee-lippen ;
   Tha bee-butts be all bare :
An' whare tha busks an' barras be,
Tie a bullbagger to tha tree,
   I zeed tha ackmals thare."

" Lord, dame, doant agg an' argy zo,
Bin' 'e wur aprilled hours ago,
   'E've creusled vur tha day ;
I niver zeed 'e zo vore-wained,
Avore tha cock-leart all wur clained,
   Zo ott's tha use vor zay."

" I don't drill time in thease gude place,
Wangéd or no, mine's tutwork pace,
   Zo ott's this hackle vor ?
Chewers báu't gwain to crick my back,
Britting o' thick an crazing thack,
   But yet I'll do my coure."

" Yer be tha voaks !   I'm glad vor zee-em,
An brórt Jan Scrape tha Crowder wi' 'em :
    Well, Gaffer Voord, how be ?
And Gammer too !   Dame, how d'ye doo ?
And Scrimmit Joe, an' lanky Loo,
    We'me cruel glad vor zee.

" An' leetle Bob ! tha daps o's veather,
(Hoi, wull, us did count on un, reather :)
    Yer Bobby yer's tha crickett,
Tha chield's avroared, tha conkerbells
Be hangin' to un—Yett theesel,
    Bob—Yen thick auther thicket.

" Ah, Bob, thee wisn't biver there,
Thee cricket kip by Granny's chair ;
    How all at home d'ye laive ?"
" Why Zukey's pinswell's going wrang,
An' Nance 's got a nimpingang,
    An' Urchy tha bone-sheave."

" Ay, wull, ther always is a summet,
Laist Zinday wi' a drap o' runnet
    I jist a junket made,
An' whe'r twur wort or mazzard pie,
Ur whe'r it wur tha junket, I
    Zem 't hurt my leetle maid."

" Why, now you mine ma, wan vornoon,
Hur mitched vro' schule, an' I'll be boun'
   Hur ait zum greenish trade.
Sloans, bullans, and haigles be about,
I'll warney now as el turn out
   'Twur they that harmed tha maid."

" Jist put her tooties in hot watter,
An' gie'r a few strang argans arter,
   Or else zum featherfowl ;
I zarve my man zo when he is sick,
Et dith more gude than kautchy vizzick,
   'Tes gude vor young an' oul' !

" Well, Giles tha hatch as well may hapse :
Cum, cum you buoys, hitch up yer caps,
   We'll try vor pick a bit.
Cum, naybors, doo dra nigh tha board,
Tha very best us can avoord—
   Cum, all know whare vor zit.

" Vreus, yer's a squab-pie ; there's a guse ;
Zum laver ; whitpot ; o't d'ye chuse ?
   Zee, yer's zum yerly chibbol.
Doant look vor lathing, limmers.   Be
Them taties cladgy ?   Rabbin, zee ;
   Doo hayt if 'e be ibble.

" Us killed a peg laist Munday, but
Tha natlings an' tha bliddy-pot
  Both turned out gude vor nort.
But howmsomdever us ded wull,
The corbetts be wi' beäcon vull,
  Bezides dree stanes o' mort.

" Doo let me help 'e, Varmer Hayl,
Vrom theäse yer dibben o' roast vayl,
  Or vrom theäse muggett pie."
" No. I've a-doo, but if 'e plaise,
I'll ha a crub wi' vinhed chaise,
  'Tis 'most too gude vor I.

" Yer, eetle Bobby's plate's aslat ;
Till un a traunchard vrom tha tack
  Wi' zum nice doucet pie.
Bobby, doant ait them trade o' crumplings,
Shalt ha' thee vill o' appul dumplings
  An' clotted crayme bam-bye.

" Lewy, hell Bet a cup o' zider ;
Or, Jan, thee zitt'st tha naist o' zide her,
  And doattiest 'pon tha gurl.
Why, buoy, art bosky, or scootchy-pawed ?
Thee'st slottered all thee drink abroad,
  Ott maks tha luke sa thurl ?

" Ther's Lew a-glinting at thy maid !
I marvel Lewy isn't vraid,
　　Thee'rt zich a stuggy brute :
Why ott dith luke sa gallièd vor ?
Tha luve that hath a jillus mor'
　　'll bear a bitter vruit.

" I'll warn, thee neesn't vear o' Bess,
Her used vor slammocky hur dress,
　　Bit now hur frap'th up tight ;
Hur used vor ha' a poochy way,
But now hur's mostly peart an' gay,
　　Laist Re-el set her right.

" Lawks, good-now, naybors, hav 'e din ?
I sem 'e 've hardly yit begen."
　　Ees, ev'ry squinch es vull :
Jist now es veelt unkimmon leary,
I'm glitted now wi' vaisting weary,
　　So ait na moor I wull."

" Wull, if 'e 've din, zay grace out loud,
An', Janny Scrape, go get tha crowd,
　　And crowd a merry toon !
Dame Voord 'll sng a bit 'ner chair,
An' Gaffer p'raps 'll snoozle wi' 'er ;
　　We'll daunce in t'other room.

"Bit now I think ou't, on tha plaunchin',
Our veet'll zet et all a-scraunchin',
 Go zwaip tha zand away ;
Giles, git a mite o' rubbly cawl
They've drawed a wallage on o' small,
 'T 'as smeetchéd all tha day.

"Now let it blunk, us ban't afraid
Poor Bobby's hands wi' cold be spraid,
 Don't scrap 'em to tha vire,
A derrymouse might nest wi' you,
And snooze away tha winter dro'
 An' not vor spring desire.

"Jim is all reart ?   Now, Scrape, thee toon !
Nelly, my chuckie, mainy to 'un,
 And tell un ott vor crowd !
Cum, hands acrass, tha middle down,
An' up again.   War wing ! turn roun',
 I'm in a parfick soud.

"Us ha' a kintry daunce sa sil'm,
I be a'most a-choked wi' pilm,
 Do gie's a drap o' trade !
When 'e be tired o' dauncing, try
A game o' bunky bean bam-bye,
 Or let us bunky Ned.

" How menny vingers do 'e zee ?
Darney, 'tis dimmit all ta me,
 I dinnaw wher I'm gwain ;
Kip ma tha vire an' winder vrom,
Why wher' be all tha voaks a-gone ?
 Ther's noan be yer, 'tis plain.

" I've beed a quarter be tha watch,
Oh, lawks ! I've trad upon a patch,
 I'm veared a shall go scat ;
The plaunching's lick a gliddered pond,
I used o' blindy-buff be vond,
 But I must zee, that's vlat !

" Ah ! I ha' cotched tha ! If 'e plaise '
'Tis pudgy Will. I've lost ma paise,
 But 'it I'll hould en vast.
Darney ! et es na use vor pote
Er tussell zo. I've vound 'e out,
 And you'll be bunked ta last.

" Et mak'th a pusky chap vor blow,
I oughdn't ta be pussed up zo ;
 Et made ma amost mazed :
I moody hearted got to be,
Jist as a poked ma hand on thee,
 I wur most nation taysed.

" I zee, Jim's tired o' this yer sportin',
He'd zoonder Nelly Brown be courtin',"
   " Her's vit vor live ta town ;
I'd rayther awn her purty mou'
Than ha' our mewstead's beggest mow
   Or vang up veevety poun' ".

" Well, Jim, to tak' her at thy waartin,
Thee kisn't think to ha' 'er, that's sartin ;
   So pitha, tell na more ;
Dwellin' o' maids thee kisn't ha',
'll werritt all thee loive away,
   An vill thee brow wi' vores.

" Nor welgars, no nor withy bans,
'll vix ther herts ner bin' ther hans,
   When all sems gwayin' suaut,
Jist when 'e sem 'e've schuled ther hart,
An' a' yer awn's a-gettin' sart,
   Yer schollard rin'th a-truant.

" I've zeed a power o' nice young wimmen,
But cum vor knaw mun an' what be mun,
   The chits be leetle vally ;
Avore I'd be as I've a-beed
I'd 'stead of daysent niching reed
   Dra' popples wi' a Malley.

" Bet zee, they be tha pawns a-draying,
An' harkee ! ott's our Bess a-zaying ;
    Tha awner o' thick thing
Mus' kiss tha velly o' tha butt,
An' on tha sharp a dashell put
    Avore 'a hath es ring."   ·

Away Dick rin'th.   Now vor tha naist
Mus' grip es maid around ur waist,
    An' tak' ur to tha barn,
An' shet tha curt an' gurden geats,
An' stay vor wimb a strik' o' wets,
    An' gie tha maid tha carn.

" 'Tis Jim an' Nelly Brown !   I warn
Jim's not o'er queck vor wimb tha carn,
    Well, niver min'.   Let's yer!"
" Tha next v'ra turn o' hood mus' laid
'S gurl to tha linhay in tha mead,
    An' kiss a yaw that's ther'."

" O lawks ! 'tis little Bobby.   Whuse
Thee maid, Bob ? queck, cheeld, 'ich dith choose."
    " Is Granny Voord in rume ?
I doant lick gurt axwaddle Sal,
Nor pimping duggytratty Mal,
    Gran's worth a dizzin o' em."

" Yer's Jim an' Nell ! (all auver doust ;)
Why, Nell, thee handkecher's a-foust,
  Ott vor dith luke sa wist ?"
" 'Tis thick gurt huuk.   I tell 'e all
Auver tha passou's desk I'll vall
  Avore I wool be kist."

" Law, Nell, doant quarley, 'tis bet fun,
I zem Jim Barrow's lick ma sun ;
  Ye'll ziug anither tune
Avore the braun's a-burned again ;
I'll warn yer vust rewtratter's gwain,
  Fegs I'll be gossip to 'un.

" I 'sure 'e Jim's no drumbledrane,
Drashel an' mattick 's all tha zame
  T' he, —'s a likely lad ;
A beat'th mun all vor hack an' hail,
An' if he shar'th yer feather-pail
  Ye needu't be o'er zad.

" Yer Vaarmer Voord, wher be ?   Ya knaw
Jim always was my dollylaw.
  Cum, us be wull to-do ;
We've yarned anew' vor ectle Bob,
I want 'e build vour waalls o' cob
  Vor thaise yer purty two."

" Wi' all ma hert.   Ees, Jim an' Nell
E've zarved yer Dames an' Maisters well,
     And yer rayward shall vend ;
I'll gie tha 'ouse, hoy, an' hadge roun' ;
Smaal-acker Close vor gurden groun',
     An' proud to caal th'a vrend.

" Jim's jist tha chap as I admire,
* FRANK BERRY'S BUKES mak' menny a 'Squire.
     They can't yet mak' a man ;
Thee'st din thee dooty all thee live,
Now do thee dooty to thee wive—
     Nelly gie Jim thee hand.

" And naybors all, 'tis gitting neart,
So, Giles, go geese ould Brock up teart,
     Jim, zee all shore an' sartin !
An' thees day month, if all be well,
Our Jim, plaise God, 'll marry Nell—
     All meet ta Whitveel Bartin."

---

* Francis Berry was long the chief steward of the North
Devon landlords. His "bukes" held, consequently, the great
claim to squiredom.

PEART II.

Scene out ta Whitvecl Bartin.

WELL, Grace, my banns be out to-day,
  Jim has a'reddy bin' vor zay,
    'Tis cruel hard vor wait.
Lawks, Varmer Voord's a-trattin in
Wi' Dame Voord (bless hur mappet chin) ;
    They'm close ancest the yeat.

" O, Gracey ! I be all ageest,
Ott be mun cum vor ? I've a-guest !
    Oh—I'm sa timmersom'."
" Now doant make-wise an' fincy zo,
Yer galdiment must zoon be go,
    Vor yer is Jim a-cum.

" How nice a look'th wi's brau new coat
An' bits o' buoy's-love stickt in to't ;
    Oh ! ott a sight o' vlowers !
Sweet butter-rosems, gooly cups,
Whit-zindays, snap-jacks, goosey vlops,
    An' baisiers too in pours.

" Pollyantice an' Cuckoo too i' fegs,
Lent roses, withy-wind, butter 'n eggs,
 Yew brimmel too sa early,
Zayhaddick, that vine harb vor hosses,
Zarreth to kip us all vrom crosses,
 Zoursalves, an' hiles o' barley.

" Well, Jim, how be ?   Urn in man, urn !
Doant stand drabreeching to tha durn,
 Bit step wayin tha zell.
Play vore thy leg min.   Pithee spaik,
Or else poor Nelly's hart'll braik—
 Why doant 'e spaik to Nell ? "

" Nelly, tha day's a-cum ta-last,
When us twain 'll be linkt up fast :
 I zim'd 'twid niver cum :
Ees fegs, I thort my nits wur deeve,
Zaid I, ' Od zooks, I can't beleeve
 I shall carr Nelly haum.'

" Thees morn I yeard the gladdies zing,
And drishes too lick enny thing,
 I thort my heart 'd bust ;
A reed-mote 'd a-knact ma down
Thort I, zo zweet wur ivry zoun'
 When I zeed Nelly rust.

" Bet now, I zem I cou'd laype owre
Guennever pool or Mar'od tower ;
 Ees fey, I zem, I be
Sa lissom an' sa limber, Grace,
That if thee shaw'st that purty face,
 Fath, I shall towsell thee !

" Bit yer cums Maister." " How beè, Nell ?
Ott's matter, Gracey b'ant hur well
 Nan ? is our Nell apurt ?"
" Tha frump o't Varmer, as may zay,
Hur layv'th us all, 'e zee to-day,
 An' veelth a littul hurt."

" Pitha, git out ! No looking down,
Jim dithn't car 'e in ta town,
 Ye'll ha a varmeric loive ;
'Tis Lime-ash vloor an' a cob-wall'd home,
But thof yer cheney 'll be cloam
 He'll mak th' a happy woive.

" I've zeed voaks clapped in manor-houzes
Wi' herts no bigger than a lowzes,
 And knawed the pimpin'st place
Wi' bowerly maids, an' vore-right men ;
The gurt-house shou'd a' be vor them,
 They wid tha Manor grace.

   b

" Well, how d'ye fadge, Nell ?—better ? hoy ?
Cum dress, maid, e'll be late bam-bye,
   Do, Gal, as 'e be bidden."
" Lawk, Voord, doant werrett.   How d'ye try ?
(Wan drap o' gommer-margery,
   'E ke'pt'h on zich a lidden.)

" Ay, wull, I thort hur'd crickle-to ;
Now, Jim, jist while tha maids be go,
   I must commerce wi' thee—
When 'e be jined, thof things go wraugy,
Not e'en the passon can untang'e,
   Zo strive vor both agree.

" Thee'st got thy latch Nell vor thee woive,
I know thee lov'st her as thee loive,
   I ausney zich a farra' !
But, Jim, doant dra thee stroile away,
The shetlake that rin'th out to-day,
   Can grind no grist ta-marra.   ·

" I mind an alkitotle o't
Avore a month had got a-quot
   How us did documenty !
'Tis ninnyhammer's work I zay,
To graunge an' guddle all tha day,
   Being gude things be sent 'e.

" Nell isn't a gurt fustilugs
O' cart-hoss heft, an' hulking dugs,
   Hur shant be pauched about,
Tho' thee'rt in desperd haydigees
Doant flerry Nell. But by degrees
   Ha thee vull shillard out.

" Hey, yer hur com'th vor pruve her truth ;
Hur zmell'th ta me like elder blooth."
   " Oh, Nelly, my dare Nell,
Vrom all the worl' were I to chusy,
'Twid still be thee. I widn't cusey,
   Vor Queen Victoria's sel'.

" Stap ! Ot's the dringet ta the door ?"
"Up vour-an'-twenty maids an' more,
   Dame dithu't zem tha fuss ;
But they've a strubb'd vlower knats an' heaths,
And fudgeed up zum purty wreaths
   To waalk ta church way us.

" Ees, there is burly-faced Jan,
And Urchy Thorn's bonehealthing's gau,
   Or layv'd behind ta Bartin ;
And Joe an' Will have each a-bro't
A main peart o' the leet they've got,
   Gosh 'e'll ha quite a vortin.

" Urchy, 'th a-made 'e pair o' crooks,
Jocy codgloves an' copperclouts,
    Vor when 'e vreeth tha hadge ;
And leetle Bob 'th bro't Nell zum daffer
A new-fardelled Bible vrom es Gaffer,
    A velling plough an' a dradge.

" An' Bobby 'th vaught 'e vor es sel'
Haimses, a hanniber, a vell,
    A drapper vor tha calves,
A barker, barraquail, a bittle,
A ribb an' cheesewring.   That's no little ;
    Bob dithn't gie by halves.

" Us wur betwitting Bob to-day,
Vor gieing all es things away,
    Begummers, us wur cort.
Akether, ' bin ma kit's ago,
I can't work w'e'r I wull or no,
    I'll maunch an' drink vor nort.'

" But, Jim, I've tould 'e bit tha carning ;
Dame, gie's a morgt vor thy house-waarming,
    Thee needst git leet' thysel',
An elsh vourpost wi' vittings prapper.
A few Welsh flannin' vor a flapper,
    A bed-tye, too, vor Nell.

" Dame send'th, too, a skillet, cowal, an' trundle,
A kieve, o' pillor-drawers a bundle,
   Tay dishes, keigers, waiters,
Zum inkle, gurts vor bliddypots,
A latten lantern, stales vor mops,
   A standard, an' four heaters.

" Two carmantrees, a pony-saddle,
Witch ellem limbers vor mewstaddle,
   Amost tha courtlage vull ;
A seedlip, scuffle, skerryflier,
Saltrees an' whink vrom Varmer Dyer,
   Way use of his prime bull.

" A two-bill, tichcrook, an' tormentor,
Gude when vor burn tha pile 'o ventur',
   A piler, an' paddle iron,
A pair o' kittibats, an' gallaces ;
They was, gudenow, es puir buoy Wallis's.
   All thaise vrom Varmer Hiern.

" But more an' that, I'm towl'd by Gaffer
To gie tha Sparkie, that prime yaffer
   That's down in Goiley mead ;
An' I've a-zent to thee pegs' looze,
Vrom my laist farra' two young zows ;
   I'm glad they wasn't speyed.

" My ould asneger 'll doo vor put
Into a little gurry butt,
 That Varmer Voss has sent 'e ;
An' girts, a guidestrap, hayvor seed,
A gaff, dree picks vrom Varmer Reed,
 An' two gude zoles (wan's plenty !")

" Ould, northering, gurbed, hadge-tacker, Dick,
Hath brort (I zed 'twas lick-a-to-lick)
 Dree pearts o' Dick's awn yusen ;
Skeerings o' wormeth, tweeny legs,
Clum, limp'skrimp, velvet docks, so Fegs,
 I'd burn it, bit doant refuse-'en."

" Stap, stap, I yer a dap ta door,
I thort the oss 'd bin avore,
 Poor ould piobaldish thing !
Doant creem me, Nell, nor sem unwillin' ;
Git up by Jim, tap o' the pillin' ;
 James, hav' 'e got tha ring ?"

" Jim, we'll jist ha' a dash-an-darras."
" No, Voord, 't'll mak' en auver dairous,
 I want ha' Nelly dered."
" I'm drow, 'tes buldering, Dame, ta-day.
No geowering Voord, mind ott I zay,
 Or I shall be afeared.

" 'S a longful while a-muving vore,
They'll be ta latter lammas zure,
 Ould Brock's a gittin' gastable ;
I want vor zee 'e clear an shear,
Gie Brock a whop, Jim, while 'e 'm yer,
 I wad a-be to Bastable.

" There, lick two culvers they'm a-go ;
Gracey, yen arter 'em thee shoe,
 And broodle o' tha day,
When Radgy Vuzz or Rabbin Knapp,
Or zum more weather-lucker chap
 'll help thee to unray.

" Dame, 'e've a-tiched a allernbatch,
Ye'm always diddling o' my latch,
 You doant min 'ott 'e zay.
'Twas don an doff all droo tha spring,
An' now I be a davered thing,
 An' not young Gracey Gray.

" Cou'd my poor chumber coander spaik,
'Twid zay my hart ed lick to braik
 A creudling auver's letters ;
Till wau day, tachy, hackled, forth,
I zed more tears they wasn't worth,
 An' brock mun all ta flitters.

" Why did 'a all tha zummer bother
Me wi' 'es tutties an es vlother,
    A-daggling arter me ?
But there, I be a-telling doil,
Ott dith et argy Dame to roil ;
    There's noan, I zem, like he !

" Vump goeth my hart if Robert frown,
Aw, do 'e strive vor much-en-down,
    They zay 'a Tamsin coorts ;
There's nort bit leather-birds be flying,
Larks be turned windles, Love goeth sighing.
    Lawks !   Rab zo put to's shourts.

" Zarch tha whole worl', vrom Guenever
To Squier Mules' ta Muddever,
    Moot iv'ry brack about un:
But thof us doant jist now agree,
Nort Dame shall bock ma luve vor he,
    'Tis 'n unket e'th way-out un."

" Lawks, doant be clummed by Rabbin Knapp,
'Sa bibbling, boostering, brinded chap,
    A dinderhead hadge-boar !
Begorsey ! vor a coager's en',
I'll till 'e vievety better men,
    Rab was made backsevore.

" 'Sa got a whargle in es eye,
An 's a parfick rames v'rall's sa high,
 Isn't ha ramaking !
An' then 'es swinkum swankum waälk,
An' taffety dildrums in es tälk,
 Rucky ta zich a thing !

" A lubbercock gurt wangery toad,
'A niver carr'th but half a load,
 Tha quirking fule's two-double ;
A panking, pluffy nestledraff,
'e'm too good haveage vor'n by haff,
 Ha isn't worth zich trouble.

" Let un take Tam'sin to es mixen,
'A trap'th wi' thick stayhoppin' vixen,
 Her's trignomate now to 'nn,
Good honest voaks shid kibbits keep,
Ta wallop all zich mangy sheep ;
 You shan't, Grace, edge a croom.

" Why, if ha lik'th ta walve in mux,
Let un ward in it to es hux,
 Droo iv'ry hole an' drang ;
If ha lov'th jaques, why let un beckon,
Hagegy Bess; wi' zich, I reckon,
 Ha now delight'h vor mang.

" Had 'e bin always iteming,
A flittering, coltree, giglot thing,
  'A might a-flinked 'e vrom en ;
The tilty, twily, preckett toad,
'A striv'th vor stample 'e abroad ;
  Soce ! why do 'e dwell on en ?"

" Aw, Dame, doant beysle'n all tha day,
Vor I be dunch to all 'e zay,
  I luve en as ma loive ;
O, es shall belve vrom hour ta hour,
Ur blake away avore es door,
  If 'a mak'th Tam es woive."

" Doant zoundy now zoaks, vor yer be
The voaks back wi' tha woodquists. Zee !
  Poor Nelly'th got the flicketts.
I zee, Joe Routley's maximing ;
I mind, I blished lick enny thing,
  Zich times they wull be wecket !"

" Yer Dame us be ! The job's a-doo !
Vor wull begun es best peart droo,
  Eute all a mug o' ale ;
Take, soce, a sliver as a nummett,
Jimmy, your Missus wanty'th zummett,
  Ur look'th as if her'd quail."

" Me ?   Varmer Voord, I ban't amiss,
But I can't hulder haff zich bliss,"
    " Nelly, in this yer nappy ;
I wish th' a merry honey-mune,
Grace—be all zingle married zoon,
    And all tha marri'd happy !

" And now we'd better all make haste
Ta Barracott's tha weddin' vaist,
    Zo let us muve along ;
We'll ait thur mait, thur ale we'll quaff,
Till they vorgit in happy laugh
    That weddin' days be long."

PEART III.

Scene out ta Barracott.

"FEGS, Nelly, 'twill be veeveteen year,
Naist Zinday zennett, we've be yer,
Es voot Time spraddl'th fore ;
An' tho' es sive bet lightly vall,
'E dithn't fail ta skeer down all,
'E dithn't skip a vore.

" Dear Varmer Voord, an' Dame not yer !
An' their poor cracky lie-a-bier !
There's Dame an' Maister's chair ;
Wi' thick I zem they bâ'nt a-go,
I hear ' Jan Anderson my Jo,'
An' zee tha ould pair there.

" Plum be tha zoil a-tap their breast ;
May nort vrom out their place o' rest
Less zweet than vi'lets spring ;
May sexton's shoul, or ploughman's vell
Hulve not wan turf where they two dwell—
Their grute's a holy thing.

" Let's hope Death's mapot is a-clit,
Ha zurely wan't clunt more o's 'it,
   Tha bell won't always doll ;
Et auffen wulv'th wi' merrier noise.
(Honey ! we've got two purty buoys,
   Peart-an'-parcel of our soul ! ")

" Ees, bit jist now voaks lie in swars,
Guns niver blast in ould Death's wars,
   Ha zoon vill'th up es stroll :
Tha cocker'd cheeld, tha doylish chun,
Bushed or unbushed, if Death jet'th one,
   Ha must obey es call.

" Zum buckle vor a lang time wi'en,
An' zum sluze down an' niver creen ;
   Zum git a rudderish nudge,
Wi' zum 'a hold'th a lang corrosying,
Wi' ithers not an hour's a-cosing,
   No dawdling, they must budge.

" Radge Fuzz went slap-dash, pack an' fardel,
Chucked down by Routledge in a quardel,
   'A valled flump on a shord ;
Scummerd wi' blid, es clathers doused,
'A died wi' jeers vrom all tha house,
   He calling on es Lord."

Joe, drinking bed-ale wort next day,
Went wi' tha bellyharm away ;
 An' pumble-footed Will,
Wi' croping Church-house grules long fed,
Chammed a crume mite o' warm clit bread,
 An' made a churchyard hill.

Old Jones and Smith, two half-saved fools,
Ait gullamouths o' pixy-stools
 To kill a score enoo ;
Young litterpouchy, lop-legged Hunt
Hid Ned the michard in a bunt,
 And fairly squeezed en droo'.

The dawcock buoy, young Harry Tulk,
Was pixy-led into a pulk,
 An' there we found en dead ;
Drink had begoodger'd creunting Dick,
An' a cricked his niddick way a pick,
 Which made Dick gook his head.

At Varmer Voss, ta Comb's, gurt survey,
A tut turned young Giles topsey turvey,
 An' rump a-cum on tha vad ;
Two buoys at their gammets in a brake,
One's sparrabled shoes kicked tither's neck,
 Tha horseplay killed tha lad.

Suke died to grubby Sam's upsetting
A-cause her aller wanted letting,
　　Or jist a soak in barm ;
Ould Tom tha tucker was strick by dinder,
Es clibby-mouth buoy vàlled out o' winder,
　　Down ta Hulsander Varm.

Stiverpowl George, wi' th' aigle tooth,
That lerrupped Blake vor kissing Ruth,
　　Was broached by Gommer's bull ;
A blunk o' vire skrent Chrisemore Nan ;
Buddled in 's drink was runty Jan,
　　Tha hesk es mostly vull.

Doan sheets cawed poor Want-catcher Ned,
They didn't coalvarty es bed
　　Down ta tha ' Bunting Tups ;'
A slinnaway stram vrom Balsden's evil
Sent Cat-handed Huphrey to tha ——,
　　Vor all es chucky chups.

" Law ! massy Jim, ot kautch be tellin',
On ivry shammock 'e be dwellin',
　　Let's cuff another tale ;
Vrom 'limbick thee shalt ha' a gill,
O't do 'e think o' leetle Will ?
　　I zem 'a looketh pale.

Which is tha sherpest, he or's brither?
Eart wan I zem, an eart the t'ither,
 I gied mun out to-day;
Freyed ribbins, and ticfil'd rattletraps,
An' in mun tha dear little chaps
 Their rabberts did array.

Ott a cawbaby Jimmy is—
But 'it ta day es blid wur riz,
 Gale-headed Jones, ta Cleve;
Was playing maxims upon Will,
An' made tha little fellow squeal,
 'A did es halse-nits theeve.

Says Jim, " Jones, you've condiddled they,
Just in your huggermugger way,
 Cum, yen mun back agen."
With that Jones hull'd out a kern—
" Co, Co," says he, " I've you to learn,"
 An' chawed up close to Jim.

Jim floshed up, " I shan't bate, or 'it
Ha' stewers wi' you or 'it your kit,
 Jist gie our Bill his right,
Or ha' this quickbean on thy back."
Wi' that Jones gied hissel a tack,
 An' axed Jim if he'd fight.

" Jim looked tha chounting chap ta paise,
Then ran agen en way a vaise,
 An' mauled en sure anew ;
'A zoon tann'd out o'en es condudle,
An' zent en on tha quar'l ta broodle,
 Making zich a to-do !

" There's nort to Jimmy lik' es brither,
How they doo clitch to wan anither,
 Jist like two chucky-cheeses !
Lang may their youthful redeship grow,
And be their station high or low,
 As Gód A'mighty plaises.

" Jim had to-day a gurt disaster,
'A brock a quar'l o' glass, an's Maister
 Gie'd en the custis vor't;
Et squashed tha chill-bladder on's hand,
An' home a-cum wi's vingers scrammed—
 Jim shant be whopped vor nort."

" Dowl take tha lamiger Methodie !
'T'ill be zum hinderment ta he,
 I'll dudder en wi' noise ;
Ees, Nell, Jimmy shall layve that schule,
I'll drash tha back o' tha crippledy vule,
 I'll back en 'vore es buoys."

" Jim, that cloam buzza wi' two handles,
'E bought laist vair ta Maister Randal's,
    Was tored abroad to-day ;
Giles chucked at Jan Peart's head a gammer,
Jan drawed a coping stone, a strammer,
    And I o' coose must pay.

" I can't abide, Jim, they two men,
I leathered Giles to tha true ben, .
    Gurt chuckle-headed toad ;
Tha crime o' the country go'th that Jan
Hath bin too gurt wi' drooling Nan—
    Hur's vaaling all abroad."

" Hur dith sem slagged.   Tha trapes mus' go,
Jan's wraxling ginged tha wildego ;
    Yer's a brave briss an' herridge !
Tha diddlecum toads.   I thort I glimpsed
Jan slinge to tha rebeck i' the dimpse—
    Ott must et be—a marri'ge ?

" Niver min' they.   Yer's Will an' Jim.
Well, ducksey dooseys, wher've 'e bin ? "
    " Pickin-a-rabberts' meat, Mo'r,
Crowtoe, an' Charlock, an' Caul-leaves,
Cowslop an' Cock-grass.   Ban't us thieves ?
    Will hath es breeches tor'.

" Where Coonie gut by tha shord turns roun',
Close by tha stickle-path us foun',
   In a haymaiden bush,
These corniwillius, an' in tha cliver
A copperfinch an' hoop's nest. O my iver,
   Tha leetle wans all flush ! "

" Will ! you 'bide in, I'll mend thy breeches ;
Jim go and zarch vor angletwitches
   An' blackworms vor tha burds ;
Cubabys be good, an' maskills too,
Oakems, ticks, longcripples 'll do ;
   Kip min' in bits o' shurd.

" D'ye mind ? tha flaw blawed to tha tallet,
A skirdevil or 'ot they call it."
   " No, 'twas a wash-dish, Jim,
Poor leetle pixy, wi' the tripes
'E pored down es poor oozle pipes,
   'E made es peeper tin'.

" Be dodding, Will ? Why, iss 'e must ;
Here, chiel's a nudge o' kissing-crust
   After thy leeky broth :
I've warmed thy porridge on tha trivet,
Jimmy, zay prayers avore 'e have it,
   And doant 'e slat tha clath."

" Well, James, tha buoys be in their beds,
God bless their purty leetle heads!
   I laive mun all to Him ;
I ask His blessing night an' day,
An' this, my dear, is all I zay,
   May they be like my Jim."

" An' zo they be. I zay ta Betty,
They've been gude children vrom the tetty,
   Not fulshin' wan anither.
I've all my latch. Jimmy's like you,
An leetle Will, 'tis Gospel true,
   Grows up jist like his brither ! "

" Nell, d'out the light. I zem tha e'enin',
Tha blessed hour 'vore candleteenin'
   'S the loveliest peart o' life :
I sometimes wish tha toiling sun,
Like me, when 'es day's wark wis done,
   Could zit down wi' 'es wife !

" Wan flinkett cast a top tha yeath,
Seems to throw out a loving breath,
   Which Winter's self would dove,
Even age, when creudling by home's fire,
Warms up agen wi' young desire,
   An' thinks o'er years o' Love.

"Now, as I hear tha pendalow
O' Maister's clock tick to an vro',
   I zem, 'Well, there is past
Another moment spent wi' Nell,
Let us enjoy love's moments well,
   While tha sweet blessings last !'

"A man an's wife, not stocks an' stones,
Must vall down on their dolly-bones,
   An' bless tha God who gives !
What *have* I done to 'sar such bliss,
Dear Nell, as is in wan sweet kiss ?
   'Tis worth a dizzen lives.

"A thousan' happy fancies dring,
To paint tha blossoms of my spring,
   But now I zem I've learned
Ould age don't scrimp wan single bliss,
Nor dubb tha rapture o' wan kiss,
   Wher love's once fully kerned.

"Lawk ! ot's a cockle here an' there ?
'Tis but a channel vor love's tear,
   Tha montering o' the dove ;
Mayhap zum foreward, fustling youth
Chuse vor tha fob, and vor tha smooth :
   But this, Nell, isn't love !

" Love isn't a mere simathin'
Begaiged wi' bloo' o' lips or skin,
   Or person short or tall ;
'Tis vor a kindred soul ta sigh,
With it ta live—without it die ;
   'Tis this, or nort at all.

" 'Tis well enoo vor lips to meet,
'Tis sweet—I own 'tis cruel sweet,
   I don't zich things disparage ;
But when a heart weds way a heart,
When soul weds soul they'll niver part,
   Vor this is heavenly marri'ge.

" An' surely, Nell, zich luve is ours,
An' zo we'll pass our earthly hours,
   While we together dwell ;
That when in tha bright ways above,
Two spirits fly still joined in Love,
   They'll zay, ' THAT'S JIM AN' NELL.' "

Glossary

OF

DEVONSHIRE WORDS.

MEM.—The chief object of the foregoing story is to interweave every provincial word known to the Author; and he has kept this object in view so closely that few verses have been added during the progress of the tale without the introduction of at least three or four new words. This may have, in many instances, interfered with the poetical interest of the tale, but will, it is presumed, increase its local value. The Author is not aware of any composition formed on a similar plan, and he must reiterate that the object of the story of "Jim and Nell" is to string together, not merely the county pronunciations, but the idioms and the provincialisms of the Devonshire dialect.

A. The letter a precedes many adverbs without much qualifying their meaning.

A-bear, ⟩ v. to endure, to put
Abide, ⟩ up with.

Acker, s. acre.

Ackmal, s. nuthatch.

Afeard, ad. afraid.

Ageest, aghast, terrified.

Agging, egging on, raising quarrels.

A-gin, or Agen, ad. against, near to.

Ago, gone, past, ex. "jist ago," nearly dead.

Aiggle-tooth, s. double-tooth, (qy. aiguille tooth, sharp tooth.)

Akether, quoth he.

Alkitotle, s. silly elf.

All-abroad, open.

Aller, s. a pinswell.

Allernbatch, s. an old sore (qy. an aller blotch).

An, than, ex. "more an' that."

A-nan (see Nan), say it again.

Aneest, anear, near (close a-neest, next to).

Angletwitch, s. an earthworm, baitworm.

An't, am not.

Aprilled, *a.* soured.

Apurt, *ad.* pouting, out of temper.

A-quott, *a.* a-squat, squatted, weary of eating.

Arg, }
Argify, } *v.* to argue, to dispute.

Arish, *s.* stubble, ground fit for the plough.

Aslat, *ad.* cracked as an earthen vessel.

Asneger, *s.* an ass.

A-top-o', on the top of, on.

Ausney, *v.* to augur, to anticipate.

Avore, *adv.* a-fore, before.

Avroar, *ad.* frozen, frosty.

Ax, *v.* to ask.

Axwaddle, *s.* a waddling unwieldy woman.

Azoon, *adv.* soon.

Backsevore, *ad.* wrong-sided.

Baisiers, *s.* auriculas.

Bak, *v.* to beat.

Bam-bye, by-and-bye, soon.

Ban't, am not.

Barker, *s.* a whetstone for scythes.

Barm, *s.* yeast.

Barra, *s.* barrow, a gelt pig.

Barraquail, *s.* a spreader, to prevent traces touching horses' heels.

Bartin, *s.* Barton, a large farm.

Bate, (*qy.* contraction of debate) *v.* to contend, to quarrel.

Be, *part.* been. Ex. " I've a be up to aunty's."

Beat, *s.* peat, the spine or turf.

Bed-ale, *s.* ale brewed for conviviality at a birth.

Bed-tye, *s.* a bed.

Bee-butt, *s.* beehive.

Bee-lippen, *s.* beehive (*qy.* the lip or aperture of a hive).

Been, *s.* a band or twisted twig.

Begayged, *ad.* bewitched.

Be-goodgerd, *ad.* bedevilled.

Begorsey, a little oath.

Begummers, a little oath (*qy.* by grandmother).

Being, because. Ex. Being 'tis so.

Bellyharm, *s.* the colic.

Belve, *v.* to bellow.

Ben, idiom " to the true ben," to the full purpose.

Be-scummer, *v.* to smear.

Bettermost, *a.* best.

Betwit, *v.* to upbraid.

Beysled, *ad.* beastlied, dirtied, demeaned.

Bibble, *v.* to bib, to drink, to tipple.

Bide, *v.* to abide, to stay.

Billéd, (*qy.* Bullhood) *ad.* distracted.

Bin, because.

Bittle, *s.* a large wooden hammer.

Biver, *v.n.* to shake.

Blackworm, *s.* a black beetle.

Blast, *v.* to explode, " blast i' the-pan," to miss fire.

Blake-away, *v.* to faint.

Blid, *s.* blood, blid an' ouns, blood and wounds, an oath.

Bliddy-pot, *s.* black pudding.

Blindego, *s.* a short-sighted person.

Bloggy, *ad.* sullen (*qy.* blocky, unmoveable).

Bloo', } *s.* blossom, bloom.
Bloothe, }

Blowsy, *a.* red-faced.

Blunk, *s.* a spark of fire.

Blunk, *v.* to snow.

Board, *s.* the table spread for meals.

Bock, *v.* to hinder.

Bolt, *v.* to swallow food without chewing it.

Bonehealthing, *s.* inflammation in the bones.

Bonesheave, *s.* rheumatism.

Boostering, *ad.* labouring busily, flustering.

Bosky, *ad.* tipsy.

Bowerly, *ad.* blooming, comely.

Boyslove, *s.* the plant southernwood.

Brack, *s.* a flaw.

Brake, *s.* a thicket.

Bran, *ad.* quite.

Brandis, *s.* a triangular frame to support the kettle on the fire.

Braun, *s.* the yule or Christmas fire-log.

Brimmel, *s.* bramble.

Brinded, *ad.* sour-looking, frowning.

Briss, } *s.* breeze, dust.
Brist, }

Brit, *s.* a bruise, an indentation.

Broach, *v.* to gore.

Browse, *s.* underwood, sprouts of trees on which cattle browse or feed.

Broodle, } *v.* to brood or medi-
Brudle, } tate, to be as a child when just waking. Ex. "Purty thing it hathn't broodled yet."

Bullbagger, *s.* a scarecrow, a frightener.

Buckle, *v.* to struggle.

Buckle-to, *v.* to bend, to surrender.

Buddle, *v.* to suffocate.

Buldering, *ad.* sultry.

Bullan, *s.* a bullace.

Bunk, } *v.* to hide.
Bunky, }

Bunkybean, *s.* a game of hide and seek a bean.

Bunt, *s.* a bolting mill.

Bunt, *v.* to fight with the horns.

Burlyfaced, *ad.* rough or pimply faced.

Bushed, *ad.* bishopped, confirmed.

Busk, *s.* a calf too long unweaned.

Busker, *s.* a boy too long unweaned.

Butt, *s.* a close-bodied cart.

Butt, *adv.* suddenly.

Butter-and-eggs, *s.* jonquils.

Butter-rose, *s.* a primrose.

By goodger, an oath.

Caaling, *part.* giving public notice.

Candle teening, *s.* candle light.

Carmantree, *s.* axles and wheels without carriage.

Carry-on, *v.* to take to heart (ott mak'th 'e carry-on so?)

Cast, *ad.* condemned, found guilty, "cast in damages."

Cat-handed, *ad.* awkward.

Caul-leaves, *s.* colewort, cabbage.

Cawbaby, *s.* an awkward, timid boy.

Cawed, *ad.* diseased as in sheep.

Cawsey, *s.* causeway.

Cess, *s.* recess, corn placed in the barn in a small mow before thrashing.

Cham, *v.* to chew.

Châmer or Chummer, a chamber, a room.

Charlick, *s.* the plant treacle and mustard.

Chaunting, *ad.* taunting, jeering.

Cheese, *s.* the pile of pommage in a cider press.

Cheesewring, *s.* cheesepress.

Chet, *s.* a kitten, a small child, an insignificant person.

Chewer, *s.* a char, a small job.

Chibbol, *s.* a small kind of onion.

Chillbladder, *s.* a chillblain.

Chine, *s.* the end of a cask.

Chrisemore, *s.* an unchristened child, a poor creature.

Christling, *s.* a small wild fruit.

Chuck, *v.* to jerk, to throw.

Chucklehead, *s.* a dunderpate, a slow-witted person.

Chucky, *s.* a term of endearment.

Chucky, *ad.* cherry coloured.

Chuckycheese, *s.* seed of mallow.

Chun, *s.* a quean, a bad woman.

Chups, *s.* chops, cheeks.

Church-house, *s.* poor-house.

Cladgy, *ad.* close, cloggy, glutinous, waxy.

Clap, *v.* to place or put down suddenly.

Clathers, *s.* clothes.

Clear and shear, *ad.* quite gone, completely.

Cleve, *s.* a cliff.

Clibby, *ad.* sticky.

Climmy or clammy, viscous (cold, clammy hands).

Clint, *v.* to clinch.

Clit-bread, *s.* heavy bread, bread not raised.

Clitch, *v.* to stick to.

Clitchy, *ad.* sticky.

Clitter clatter, continuous noise as of a mill.

Clitty, *ad.* close, clotty.

Cliver, *s.* goosegrass.

Cloam, *s.* delft, earthenware.

Cloamy, *ad.* made of loam.

Clopping, *ad.* lopping, lame, limping.

Clout, *s.* a blow, a cuff.

Clouted-cream, *s.* cream raised by heat.

Clum, *v.* to pull about unseemlily.

Clum, *s.* a peat cake.

Clumebuzza, *s.* (*qy.* Cloambuzzer) an earthen pan.

Clunt, *v.* to glut, to swallow.

Clut, *ad.* glutted.

Co, Co! *int.* an exclamation.

Coager's-end, *s.* end of a cobbler's thread.

Coalvarty, *v.* to warm a bed with warming-pan.

Coauder, *s.* corner.

Cob, *s.* mud or loam mixed with straw for building.

Cobnut, *s.* a wild nut, a game with nuts.

Cock grass, *s.* plantain.

Cockered, *ad.* foolishly indulged.

Cockhedge, *s.* a quickset hedge.

Cockle, *s.* a wrinkle.

Cockleert, *s.* cocklight, dawn.

Codglove, *s.* a glove used in hedge mending.

Colbrand, *s.* smut in wheat.

Colting, frolicking as a colt.

Coltree, *ad.* playful as a colt.

Comb, or Combe, *s.* a valley between hills open at one end only.

Come, *v.* to become ripe. Ex. " Cherries be come."

Commercing, *ad.* conversing.

Condiddle, *v.* to convey away secretly.

Condudle, *s.* conceit.

Conkerbell, *s.* cock-a-bell, an icicle.

Cope, *s.* the top.

Copingstones, *s.* the top stones.

Copper-clouts, *s.* spatterdashes worn on the small of the leg.

Copperfinch, *s.* the chaffinch.

Corbett, *s.* a deep salting tub.

Cornish, *v.* to use one pipe or glass for many.

Corniwillin, *s.* a lapwing.

Corrosy, *s.* a grudge, ill will.

Cort, *ad.* caught.

Cottoning, *s.* a flogging.

Country, *s.* the strata of the earth.

Coure, *s.* a course of work, a turn.

Courtlage, *s.* the fore or back yard of a house.

Cowal, *s.* a fishwoman's basket.

Cowslop, *s.* the foxglove.

Cozing or Coosing, *ad.* loitering, soaking.

Cracky, *s.* a wren, a small thing or person.

Craze, *v.* to crack. Ex. " I've crazed the tay pot."

Crazed, *ad.* cracked so as not to ring.

Creem, *v.* to squeeze.

Creen, *v.* to complain, to pine.

Creusling, *ad.* complaining without cause.

Crewdle, *v.* to gather up yourself. Ex. " To creudle anver the vire."

Crewnting, *ad.* groaning, complaining.

Crick, *s.* a spasm in the back or neck.

Crickett, *s.* a three-legged stool, a low stool used near the fire-place (*qy.* to listen to the crickets).

Crickle-to, *v.* to bend or submit.

Cricks, *s.* dry hedge wood.

Crim, *ad.* scrimped. Ex. A crim mite o't, a small part of it.

Crime o' the country, *idiom,* common report.

Crippledy fellow, *s.* a cripple.

Crock, *s.* a large iron pot for boiling.

Crooks, *s.* bent sticks to hold a horse-load on by hooks.

Croom (*qy.* Crumb), *s.* a little. Ex. " Edge a croom"—move a little.

Croping, *ad.* griping, stingy, penurious.

Crowd, *s.* a fiddle.

Crowder, *s.* a fiddler.

Crowtoe, *s.* crowsfoot, ranunculus repens.

Crub, *s.* for crib, a crust of bread, the wooden supporters of pauiers or bags on a horse.

Cruel, *ad.* very.

Crumpling, *s.* a little knotty or wrinkled apple prematurely ripe.

Cubaby, *s.* a lady-bird.

Cuckoe, *s.* the harebell.

Cuckold buttons, *s.* bur from plant burdock.

Cuff, *v.* Ex. " To cuff a tale," to exchange stories, as if contending for the mastery.

Culver, *s.* a wood pigeon.

Cuniè, *s.* moss, the green vegetation covering a pool or well.

Cusey, *v.* to swop, to exchange.

Custis or Custie, (*qy.* the cursed stick) a schoolmaster's ferula.

Dab, *s.* an adept.

Daffer, *s.* small crockery ware.

Daggle, ⟩ *v.* to run like a
Duggle, ⟨ young child (*qy.* from doggle).

Dairous, *ad.* (*qy.* dareous) daring, bold.

Dang, *v.* a diminutive oath.

Dap, *s.* a tap, a gentle knock.

Daps, *s.* a duplicate, an exact likeness.

Dash-an-darras, *s.* the stirrup glass, a parting cup.

Dashel, *s.* a thistle.

Daver, *v.n.* to fade.

Davered, *ad.* faded, blighted.

Dawcock, *s.* (*qy.* doughcock) a silly, awkward fellow.

Dawdle, *v.* to trifle, to loiter.

Deeve, *ad.* rotten. Ex. 'A deeve nit."

Dero, *v. a.* to hurry, to frighten.

Derrymouse, *s.* the dormouse.

Desperd, *ad.* desperate, very, extremely.

Diddlecom, *ad.* half-mad, sorely teased.

Diddling, *part.* tattling. Ex. always a-diddling.

Dibben, *s.* a fillet as of veal.

Dildrums, (*qy.* Doldrums) childish nonsense. Ex. "to tell Doldrums and Buckingham Jenkins," "to talk wildly."

Dimmett, } *s.* dimlight, twilight.
Dimpse, }

Diuder, *s.* thunder.

Diuderhead, *s.* a foolish person.

Dish, *s.* a cup, as tea-dish, for tea-cup.

Dishwater, *s.* the water wagtail.

Dizzen, *s.* a dozen.

Do, *part.* done. Ex. "It's a-do," It is done.

Doan, *ad.* wet, damp.

Doattie, *v.* to dote on.

Do-city, *s.* aptness, knowledge.

Documenting, lecturing, advising.

Dodding, nodding, sleeping.

Doil, *v.* to talk distractedly. Ex. "To tell doil," to talk deliriously as in fever.

Doll, *v.* to toll. Ex. "The bell dolls."

Dollybones, *s.* the knees.

Dollylaw, *s.* a darling, one foolishly indulged.

D'on and D'off, to put on and off.

Doucet pie, *s.* sweet herb pie.

Douse, *v.* to drench.

Doust, *s.* chaff, barn-dust.

Dout, *v.* to do out, to put out, to extinguish.

Dove, *v.* to thaw. Ex. "It doveth," it thaws.

Dowl, *s.* the devil.

Doylish, *ad.* light-headed.

Dradge, *s.* a bush harrow.

Drang, *s.* a narrow passage.

Drapper, *s.* a bucket for feeding calves.

Drash, *v.* to thresh.

Drashel, *s.* a flail (*qy.* a thrashall).

'Drat, an oath.

Drawbreech, *v.* to loiter, to draggle tail.

Draxel, *s.* a threshold.

Dredger, *s.* a sprinkler, or caster.

Drill, *v.* to dribble, to drop or drain wastefully.

Drill, *v.* to dry, as a mop, by running it round (drill-time, to waste time).

Dring, *v.* to throng, to squeeze.

Dring, } *s.* a throng, a crowd.
Dringet, }

Drish, *s.* a thrush.

Drool, *v.* to drivel, to water at the mouth.

Drooling, *part.* drivelling, letting slip.

Drudge or Drudger, *s.* a teamrake.

Drow, *v.* to dry.

Drow, } *ad.* dry.
Drowy, }

Dubbèd, *ad.* blunt, flattened by blows.

Dadder, *v.* to deafen with noise, to render the head confused.

Dump, *s.* a heavy sound.

Duggytratty, *ad.* dog-trotting, short-legged.

Dumbeldrane, *s.* a drone bee, an idle person.

Dunch, *ad.* deaf.

Durn, *s.* (*qy.* doorn) a doorpost.

Earn, *v.* to give earnest.

Eart, *ad.* sometimes. Ex. "Eart one, eart another."

Ea'th, *s.* earth.

Ee, *pro.* ye.

Ees, yes.

Eet, yet.

Ellem, *s.* the elm tree.

Elong, *ad.* slanting.

Elsh, *ad.* new, fresh. Ex. "An elsh maid, a raw, uncouth girl."

En, un, or 'n, *pro.* him or it, as I told en, I bought en.

Epping-stocks, for stepping-stocks, stone steps for mounting on horseback.

Es, ise, ish, *pron.* used indiscriminately for almost any personal pronoun.

Eute, *v.* to pour out.

Evet, *s.* an eft or water vein.

Evil, *s.* a three-pronged fork.

Evor, or Evory grass, rye grass. *See* Hayfor.

Fadge, *v.* to fare. Ex. "How d'ye fadge?"

Fath, ⎫
Fegs, ⎬ in faith, truly, indeed.
Fey, ⎭

Fang or Vang, *v.* to receive, to finger, to get possession of. Ex. "I vang'd to that estate last Christmas," "I vang'd a vive poun' note."

Fardel, *s.* forrill, cover of a book.

Farmerick, *ad.* farmer-like, countryfied.

Fast, *s.* the understratum of the earth.

Feather pail, *s.* a pillow.

Fess, *ad.* licentious.

Few, *ad.* some, a small quantity. Ex. "A few broth."

Fincy, *v.* to mince, to pretend gentility.

Fitpence, *s.* fivepence.

Flanning, *s.* flannel.

Flaw, *s.* a sudden gust of wind.

Florry, *v.* to shake, to agitate, to worry.

Flickets, *s.* blushes, flushes in the face.

Flink, *v.* to shake off or out.

Flinket, *s.* a small bundle of wood.

Flitters, *s.* rags.

Flopper, *s.* an under petticoat.

Flosh-out, *v.* to dash.

Flower-nat, *s.* a flower-plot, from their being planted in shape of true lovers' knots.

Flummocks, *s.* a flurry.

Flump, *ad.* heavily.

Flushed, *ad.* fledged.

Fob, *s.* froth.

Foreward, *ad.* wilful.

Fore-right, *ad.* straight-forward, plain, honest.

Fore-weaned, cross, difficult to please.

Forth, *ad.* out of temper, not one's self.

Foust, *ad.* rumpled.

Frape,. *v.* to draw tight, to brace.

Freeth, *v.* (*qy.* wreathe) to wattle, to mend the hedge.

Freyed, *ad.* (*qy.* from "Spread") displaced as the threads of ribbon by washing or wear.

Frith, *s.* (*qy.* writh) brushwood.

From, after.

Frump, *s.* the upshot, the principal matter.

Fudge, Fudgee, } *v.* to contrive to do.

Fulch, *s.* a push, a blow.

Fump, *s.* a slap.

Fustilugs, *s.* a big-boned person.

Fustle, *s.* bustle.

Fustle, *v.* to bustle.

Gads, *inter.* an exclamation of disgust.

Gaff, *s.* an instrument with long handle used to pull furze out of the furze-rick.

Galdiment, *s.* a great fright.

Gale-headed, *ad.* heavy, stupid.

Galey, or Goiley, *ad.* damp, as ground where springs rise.

Gallaces, *s.* braces.

Gallied, *part.* frightened.

Gally, *v.* to frighten.

Gammer, *s.* a butcher's spreading stick.

Gammet, *s.* a game, a little sport.

Gammer, Gommer, Grammer, } *s.* grandmother, an old woman.

Gaffer, Gatfer, Goffer, } *s.* grandfather, an old man.

G'and, or g'ender, *v.* to go yond or yonder.

Gastable, *ad.* unruly.

Geese, *v.* to girth.

Geowering, *ad.* quarrelling.

Giglot, *s.* a female laughing or playing wantonly.

Gill, *s.* a measure, quarter of a pint.

Ginged, *ad.* bewitched. (*qy.* "gingered.")

Girt, *s.* a girth.

Girts, *s.* groats.

Gladdie, *s.* the yellow hammer.

Glidder, *s.* ice.

Glint, *v.* to look askew.

Glut, *v.* to cloy, to satiate.

Gommer-margery, *s.* a spirit distilled from dregs of beer.

Googer, *s.* the devil.

Gook, *v.* to hang down.

Gooly-cup, *s.* the flower golden cup, the buttercup.

Gooseflop, *s.* the foxglove (*digitalis*).

Gossip, *s.* a sponsor.

Grules, *s.* greaves, the dry residue of melted fat.

Graunge, *v.* to eat.

Grute, *s.* earth, stock. Ex. "He's of good grute."

Guddle, *v.* to drink greedily.

Guidestrap, *s.* a long bridle.

Gulamouth, *s.* a pitcher.

Gurbed, *ad.* splashed with mud.

Gurry-butt, *s.* a dung cart.

Gurt, *ad.* great.

Gut, *s.* a large open gutter or channel on the sea-shore.

Hack, *v.* to dig.

Hackle, *s.* anger.

Hackled, *ad.* angered.

Hadge-boar, *s.* hedge-hog.

Hadge-tacker, *s.* hedger.

Hagegy, *s.* loose, untidy.

Haigle, *s.* a haw.

Hail, *v.* to cover.

Hailingstones, *s.* roof slates.

Haimses, *s.* part of horse collar.

Halse nuts, *s.* hazel nuts.

Handsel, *s.* a gift attending a bargain or first act, as an-selling the new year, or a new purchase.

Hanniber, *s.* neck collar for horses.

Hapse, *v.* to fasten with a bolt.

Hatch, *s.* a breast-high door.

Haveage, *s.* race, lineage.

Hawbuck, *s.* (*qy.* w——o buck?)

Haydigees, *s.* frolicksome mood, high spirits.

Hayvor-seed, *s.* grass seed (*qy.* seed for hay).

Heckett, *s.* fuss.

Heft, *s.* the weight.

Hell, *v.* to pour.

Hend, *v.* to hand over, to throw.

Here-right, on the spot, instantly.

Herridge, *s.* bustle.

Hesk, *s.* a hearse.

Heymaiden, *s.* ground ivy.

Hile, *s.* the beard of barley (*qy.* the pile).

Hinderment, *s.* hindrance.

Hitch-up, *v.* to hang up.

Hoke, *v.* to wound with horns, to gore.

Holm, *s.* holly (*qy.* if local).

Honey, *s.* sweet, an endearing epithet.

Hood, *s.* wood.

Hoop, *s.* the bullfinch.

Horse-hood, *ad.* in kind.

Horseplay, *s.* rough sport.

House, *s.* room. Ex. "In t'other house," "in the other room."

Hugger-mugger, *ad.* grovelling, low, clandestine.

Hulder, *v.* to hide, to conceal.

Hulking, *ad.* large.

Hull, *v.* to dig out, to hollow.

Hulsander, *s.* the white ash.

Hulve, *v.* to turn over.

Huuk, *s.* a great lump.

Hurt, downhearted.

Hux, or Huxon, *s.* the hock bone.

Inkle, *s.* tape.

'It, *adv.* yet.

Iteming, *ad.* fidgetting, trifling.

Items, *s.* fidgets.

Jaques, *s.* filth.

Jet, *v.* to jolt, to touch in way of token.

Jiffy, *s.* an instant of time.

Junket, *s.* a preparation of milk and rennet.

Kautch, *s.* a disagreeable mixture.

Kautch, *v.* to mix disagreeably.

Keak, cake.

Keiger, a cask.

Kern, *s.* a kernel.

Kern, *v.n.* to form into substance, to curdle.

Kex, Kexies, } *s.* dry stalks ; some plants, as hemlock &c., are so called.

Kibbit, *s.* a large stick.

Kieve, *s.* a large tub used for fermenting beer.

Kissing-crust, *s.* middle crust.

Kit, *s.* a tribe, collection, gang.

Kit, *s.* a collection of tools.

Kittibats, *s.* (*qy.* kitty boots) gaiters.

Lamiger, *ad.* lame, crippled.

Lanky, *ad.* tall, thin.

Latch, *s.* a door fastening.

Latch, *s.* a fancy, a wish.

Latten, *s.* tinned plate.

Latter-lammas, late, behind time.

Lathing, *s.* invitation.

Laver, *s.* a marine vegetable.

Leary, *ad.* empty.

Leather, *v.* to beat.

Leatherbird, *s.* a bat.

Leet, *ad.* little.

Lerruping, *s.* a flogging.

Let, *v.* to lance.

Lew, *s.* the Lee.

Lidden, *s.* clack, annoying re-iteration.

Lie-a-bier, *ad.* dead.

Likely, *ad.* promising, hopeful.

Limber, *ad.* pliant.

Limbick, *s.* an alembic, a still.

Limmers, *s.* limbers, joints.

Limmers, *s.* friends, acquaintance, connections.

Limperskrimp, *s.* wild celery, sought by horses when ill.

Linhay, *s.* a shed for cattle.

Lissom, *ad.* pliant, supple, lithesome.

Litterpouch, a slovenly person.

Lock, *s.* an armlock or armful, as of hay.

Long-cripple, *s.* earthworm.

Longful, *ad.* full long, long (applied to time).

Lop-legged, *ad.* lame.

Loplolly, *a.* lounging, not firm, a great loplolly boy.

Lopsided, *ad.* one-sided.

Lout, *s.* a stupid fellow.

Lubbercock, *s.* a Turkey cock, a term of derision.

Maddick, *s.* a mattock.

Main, } v. to beckon to, to give
Mainy, } directions by action.

Make-wise, v. to pretend.

Making sich a to-do, making a fuss or disturbance.

Mallard, s. a drake.

Malley, s. a donkey, a female ass.

Mang, v. to mix, to mingle with.

Mang, ad. amongst.

Mapot, s. the maw, the stomach.

Mappett, ad. mopping. Ex. "a mappett chin."

Maskell, s. a caterpillar.

Maul, v. to touch unseemly, to handle roughly.

Maunch, v. to munch, to eat.

Mawn, wicker hamper with two handles.

Maxims, s. practical jokes, play.

Mazed, ad. mad.

Mazzard, s. a small black cherry.

Methodi', s. a Methodist.

Mewstaddle, s. a frame on which the mow is set.

Mewstead, s. place where the mows are set.

Mickled, ad. choked.

Min, or Mun, man, used contemptuously.

Michard, } s. a truant.
Mitcher, }

Mitch, v. to play truant.

Mixen, s. a dunghill.

Moody - hearted, ad. weak-hearted, dispirited.

Moot, v. to root out roots of trees.

Moots, stumps, &c.

Morgt, s. a great quantity or number.

Morr, (Maur) s. a root.

Mort, s. lard.

Mowtering, ad. moultering.

Much-en-down, v. to appease or please, by making much of. Ex. "Much down the cat."

Mun, pr. them.

Mux, s. muck, mud.

Nau, what.

Natling, s. gut tied in small knots.

Neck, s. the last sheaf of the wheat harvest.

Nestledraught, s. the last born, the clearing of the rest.

Nettle, v. to offend.

Niche, s. a bundle. Ex. a niche of reed.

Niddick, s. back of the neck.

Nimpingang, s. a whitlow.

Ninnyhammer, s. a foolish person, idiot.

Noggin, s. a quarter-pint or gill.

Nort, s. nothing.

Northering, ad. wild, incoherent.

Not-half-saved, ad. foolish.

Nudge, v. to jolt, to call attention by touching.

Nummet, } s. a luncheon, a small
Nunch, } bit.

Oakebb, } s. the cockchafer.
Oakem, }

Oozle pipe, *s.* wheezing pipe, the windpipe.

Organs, *s.* the herb penny royal.

Ort, *s.* aught, anything.

Orts, *s.* scraps, refuse.

Ott, *ad.* what?

Pack-an-fardel, *ad.* entirely, with packages and bundles.

Paddle iron, *s.* an instrument to clean the plough.

Paise, *v.* to poise.

Paise, *s.* a poise, a pair of steel-yards.

Panking, *ad.* panting.

Patch, *s.* stone seed of fruit.

Panch, ⎫ *v.* to handle in an un-
Paunch, ⎭ seemly manner.

Peart, *ad.* sharpwitted, dapper.

Pendalow, *s.* a pendulum.

Pick, *s.* a hay or pitchfork.

Pick-a-back, carrying like a pack on back.

Pig's-looze, *s.* a pigstye.

Piler, *s.* a farm instrument to remove the piles from barley.

Pillin, *s.* pillion, the behind saddle for females.

Pillor drawer, *s.* a pillow case.

Pilm, *s.* dust.

Pimping, *ad.* small.

Pinswell, *s.* a sore, a black-headed sore.

Pixy, *s.* a Devonshire fairy.

Pixy-led, *ad.* led by fairies.

Pixy stool, *s.* a fungus.

Plash, *v.* to repair or interweave the hedge.

Plaunching, *s.* wooden floor, planking.

Play fore, *v.* throw forward.

Pluffy, *ad.* not solid.

Plum, *ad.* light, soft, springy, puffy. Ex. " plum soil, plum bed."

Pollyantice, *s.* the polyanthus.

Popplestone, *s.* a pebble.

Power of, much, many.

Pudgy, *ad.* fat, thick.

Pusky, *s.* difficult of breathing.

Pote, *v.* to throw about the legs.

Pouchy, *ad.* pouting.

Pulk, ⎫ *s.* a shallow pool of
Pulker, ⎭ water.

Pumble-foot, *s.* club foot.

Prockett, *ad.* perked up, pert, self-conceited.

Quail, ⎫ *v.* to faint away.
Queel, ⎭

Quarrel, *s.* square of window-glass (*qy.* a squarel).

Quickbean, *s.* mountain ash.

Quirking, complaining.

Rabbert, *s.* a rabbit.

Rabbin, *s.* Robert.

Ramaking, *ad.* thin.

Rame, *v.* to stretch out the person.

Rames, *s.* a stretched-out or lean person.

Rattletrap, *s.* useless lumber, makeshift.

Ray, *v.* to array, to dress.

Rebeck, s. the enclosed part of a barn.

Redeship, s. trust, confidence, friendship.

Reed, s. straw unbroken by thrashing.

Reed-mote, s. a pipe of straw.

Re'el, } s. a revel, a country
Rowl, } fair.

Rewtrotter, s. a swing for infants, a cradle.

Ribb, s. an iron bow used for gathering barley.

Roil, } v. to rail.
Roily, }

Rubble, s. small lumps.

Rucky, v. to crouch.

Rudderish, ad. hasty, careless, rude.

Runt, s. one of stinted growth, a thick, short-set person.

Saltrees, s. poles fixed in a cow house to tie cattle to.

Samsawed, ad. half-cooked.

Sar, v. to deserve, to earn, to get.

Sarasing, s. a fussy preparation.

'Scant, us can't, we cannot.

Scat, v. to strike flat.

Scat, ad. flat.

Scat, s. a flat slap.

Scourey, ad. smeared.

Scoochy-pawed, ad. left-handed, awkward.

Scrammed, ad. benumbed.

Scrap, v. to burn, to singe.

Scraunch, v. to grind.

Scrimmet, ad. shrunk, shrivelled.

Scrimp, v. to curtail.

Scrummage, v. to rummage.

Scuffle, s. a farm instrument resembling a harrow.

Scummer, v. to smear, to clean indifferently.

Seedlip (pronounced Zellup), s. a wooden vessel used to contain seeds while sowing.

Sem, "I sem," it seems to me.

Settle, s. a seat including a screen.

Shag, s. a seabird.

Shammick, s. a lean miserable person or animal.

Sherd, s. broken earthenware.

Shetlake, s. a stream which feeds a shoot.

Shillard, s. a shilling's worth.

Shippen, s. a cattle stall (qy. a sheep-pen).

Shord, s. a gap in the hedge.

Shou'l, s. a shovel.

Shourts, s. shifts, contrivances.

Sight, s. a large quantity.

Simathin, s. fondness.

Simmett, s. the bottom of a sieve.

Sive, s. a scythe.

Skeer, v. to mow lightly over.

Skeerings, s. hay made in pasture land, the cuttings of a light crop.

Skaredevil, } s. a black martin
Skir, } or swift.

Skrent, ad. burnt, singed.

Slagged, ad. slackened, loose, untidy.

Skerryflier, *s.* a farm instrument used to destroy weeds in potato alleys.

Skillett, *s.* a little saucepan.

Slammock, *s.* an untidy person.

Slammocking, *ad.* untidy.

Slapdash, *s.* rough lime and gravel, a ready coating for buildings.

Slapdash, *ad.* offhand, quickly.

Slinge, *v.* to loll.

Slinnaways, *ad.* sidling, slanting.

Sliver, *s.* a slice.

Sloan, *s.* a sloe.

Slotter, *v.* to spill.

Sluze, *v.* to slide down.

Smeetch, *s.* smoke.

Snapjack, *s.* white smock, lady-smock, a flower.

Soce ! *s.* a plural in the vocative case, friends ! companions !

Soursalves, or Soursopps, *s.* sorrel.

Sparky, *ad.* spotted.

Sparrables, *s.* small nails.

Speyed, *ad.* gelt.

Spine, *s.* turf, sward.

Spire, *s.* reed.

Spraddle, *v.* to stride.

Spraid, *a l.* chapped by cold.

Squab-pie, *s.* a Devonshire pie, composed of apples and flesh.

Squarrell, or quarrell, *s.* a square of glass.

Squash, *v.* to squeeze, to burst.

Squeal, *v.* to squeak.

Squinch, *s.* a crevice.

Staff, *s.* nine feet, half a rod.

Staid, *a.* settled, confirmed.

Stale, *s.* handle of a mop or broom.

Stampled abroad, *ad.* trodden upon.

Standard, *s.* a large salting tub.

Stane, *s.* a stone pot, an earthen vessel.

Stayhopping, *ad.* giddy, wanton.

Stewer, *s.* a dust, a fuss.

Stickle, *ad.* steep, a small stream.

Stinpole, *s.* a stupid person.

Stiver-powl, *ad.* bristle-headed.

Stocked or Stooded, *ad.* immoveable, stuck as in mud.

Strake, *v.* to loiter.

Stram, *s.* a loud knock.

Stram, *v.* to knock hard.

Strammer, *s.* a great thing, a lie.

Straw-mote, *s.* a pipe of straw.

Strike, *s.* half-a-peck.

Stroile, *s.* strength.

Stroll, *s.* a narrow slip of land.

Stroyl, *s.* couch grass, or other long weed usually raked out of the soil.

Strub, *v.* to strip, to take away all.

Stuggy, *ad.* short, thick.

Suant, *ad.* even.

Sugg, *v.* to sleep.

Survey, *s.* an agricultural auction.

Swankum, *ad.* careless. Ex. " swinkum swankum walk."

Swar, *s.* the ridge of corn as it falls from the sickle.

Swathe, ridge of grass from the scythe.

Tachy, *ad.* touchy, irritable.

Tack, *v.* to slap.

Tack, *s.* a shelf.

Taffety, *ad.* delicate, nice, dainty.

Tallett, *s.* a hayloft.

Tamsin, *s.* Thomazin, a woman's name.

Tang, *v.* to tie.

Tanning, *s.* a beating.

'Taty, *s.* a potato.

Tetty, *s.* a teat.

Thack, } *pron.* that.
Thacky, }

Theeky, those.

Thick, } *pron.* this.
Thicky, }

Thurl, *ad.* thin.

Tiefil, *s.* a filament.

Tiefilled, *s.* untwisted, fringed out.

Till, *v.* to deliver over.

Tilty, *ad.* testy, soon offended.

Timmersome, *ad.* timorous, fearful.

Tine, *v.* to shut, to close.

To, *prep.* at. Ex. "to-last, at last—he lives to Barnstaple."

To-do, a-do, fuss, bustle. Ex. "Ott's this to do, for."

Tooties, *s.* the toes.

Ticherook, } *s.* implements to
Tormentor, } turn peat with.

Towsell, *v.* to towse, to handle roughly.

Trade, *s.* trash.

Trape, *v.* to walk idly.

Trapes, *s.* a slut, a sloven.

Traunchard, *s.* a trencher, a wooden plate.

Trignomate, *s.* a walking companion.

Trivet, *s.* the turn-round of a grate, a tripod.

Trundle, *s.* a salting tub.

Try. Ex. "How d'y' try, how do you get on?"

Tucker, *s.* a fuller.

Tucking mill, *s.* a fulling mill.

Tussell, *s.* a contention.

Tussell, *v.* to contend.

Toil, } *s.* a hassock.
Tut, }

Tutty, *s.* a nosegay.

Tutwork, *s.* piecework.

Tweeny logs, *s.* a weed.

Twily, *ad.* toily, troublesome.

Twobill, *s.* a tool, mattock at one end and bill (or axe) at the other.

Two-double, *ad.* bent, crooked.

Unket, *ad.* dreary, lonesome.

Unray, *v.* to undress.

Untang, *v.* to untie.

Upsetting, *s.* a christening.

Urchy, *s.* Richard.

Vad, *s.* beam of cider press.

Vang, *v.* (*qy.* to finger) to receive, to raise money.

Vaige, } *s.* the strength gained
Vaise, } in taking a leap by previously receding.

Vaught, *ad.* fetched.

Veag, *s.* ill temper, a fit of passion.

Vell, *s.* part of a plough.

Vell, *v.* to separate the turf from the soil.

Vell, to fell.

Velling plough, *s.* a plough to take off the turf.

Velvet dock, s. the verbascum.

Velly, *s.* a felloe.

Vend, *v.* to find.

Vinhed, *ad.* moulded, mouldy as cheese (*qy.* from veined).

Vitty, *ad.* fitting, proper.

Vlother, *s.* unmeaning talk, nonsense.

Vore, *ad.* forward.

Vore, *s.* a furrow.

Waartin, *s.* weighing, valuation.

Waiter, *s.* a tray.

Walve, *v.* to wallow.

Wallage, *s.* a large quantity.

Wangèd, *ad.* tired.

Wangery, *ad.* soft, flabby.

Want, *s.* a mole.

Ward, *v.* to wade.

Wardship, *s.* a wagtail.

Warn, *v.* to warrant.

War-wing ! beware, take care !

Wash-dish, *s.* a wagtail.

Weather - lucker, *ad.* better-looking.

Welgar, (*qy.* woolgar) *s.* a willow.

Werritt, *v.* to tease, to worry.

Wets, *s.* oats.

Whishful, ⎫ *ad.* dismal.
Wist, ⎭

Whink, *s.* a small machine for spinning straw ropes for thatching.

Whirgle, *v.* to twirl, to roll.

Whirgle, *s.* a twist.

Whitpot, *s.* a Devonshire mixture of milk, flour, and treacle.

Whitsundays, *s.* daffodils.

Whittaker, *s.* a species of quartz.

Whop, *v.* to beat.

Whop, *s.* a heavy blow.

Whopping, *s.* a beating.

Wildego, *s.* a harem-scarem person.

Wimb, ⎫ *v.* to winnow.
Wimby, ⎭

Winder, *s.* a window.

Windle, *s.* a field fare.

Witch elm, *s.* seedling elm.

Withe, ⎫ *s.* a willow twig.
Withy, ⎭

Withywind, *s.* the woodbine.

Wollop, *v.* to beat.

Wood quist, *s.* a wood pigeon.

Wormeth, *s.* wormwood.

Wort, *s.* new beer.

Worts, *s.* whortle berries.

Wraxle, *v.* to wrestle.

Yarreth, *s.* the Yarrow.

Yaw, *s.* an ewe.

Yeat, *s.* a gate.

Yeat, *s.* heat.

Yeath, *s.* the hearth. . .

Yeathstone, s. hearthstone.

Yeu, v. to throw, to hand over.

Yewbrimmel, s. dogrose.

Yuzen, s. a trough to feed cattle from, appended to cowhouse.

Yuzen, s. a dunghill.

Zayhaddick, s. the herb Valerian.

Zart, }
Zat, } ad. soft.

Zem, v. to seem, to seem pleased with.

Zoaks, Zooks (*qy.* God's looks).

Zole, s. a plough or plough iron.

Zounds, wounds.

Zoundy, v. to swoon.

www.ingramcontent.com/pod-product-compliance
Lightning Source LLC
Chambersburg PA
CBHW031929060726
47496CB00008BA/2776